The Olive Tree

Dedicated to the Harik family of Dhour Shweir, with hope for all the people of Lebanon.
—EM
For Celeste: all my love, and a handful of olives.
—CE

The Olive Tree
Text copyright ©2014 Elsa Marston, Illustrations copyright ©2014 Claire Ewart

Wisdom Tales is an imprint of World Wisdom, Inc.

Library of Congress Cataloging-in-Publication Data
Marston, Elsa.
The olive tree / by Elsa Marston ; illustrated by Claire Ewart.
    pages cm
Summary: Sameer's neighbors left when war came to Lebanon, but now they have returned and instead of
finding a friend to play with, Sameer meets an unfriendly girl, Muna, who confronts him about taking olives
that fall from her family's tree to his side of the wall.
    ISBN 978-1-937786-29-8 (hardcover : alk. paper) [1. Neighbors--Fiction. 2. Olive--Fiction. 3. Trees--
Fiction. 4. Lebanon--Fiction.] I. Ewart, Claire, illustrator. II. Title.
    PZ7.M356755Oli 2014
    [E]--dc23
                                                                                    2014016127
Printed in China on acid-free paper.
Production Date: July 2014, Plant & Location: Printed by 1010 Printing International Ltd,
Job/Batch #: TT14050858
For information address Wisdom Tales, P.O. Box 2682, Bloomington, Indiana 47402-2682.
www.wisdomtalespress.com

The Olive Tree

By Elsa Marston

Illustrated by Claire Ewart

✣Wisdom Tales✣

or many years the house next to Sameer's had stood empty. "What a pity!" his mother often said. The family who lived there had gone away during the troubles, because they were different from most of the people in the village. But now, thank goodness, the long war was over, and they were coming back.

  Shaded by the old olive tree, Sameer leaned on the stone wall between the two houses and watched eagerly. The neighbors were moving in, carrying everything needed to bring a house back to life.

  He didn't remember anything about the family— but wouldn't it be wonderful if they had a boy? Oh, he hoped so! Two boys could have such fun roaming the mountainsides, kicking a ball, eating ripe figs—and climbing on the olive tree.

Sameer looked up at the gnarled old branches. They were good branches for climbing—and they still bore the best olives in Lebanon. That's what his mother always said, as she prepared them in jars with lemon and salt. Sameer's family had enjoyed those olives for as long as he could remember.

The neighbors soon settled into their house. They were always polite—but they rarely said more than a few words, and they never returned visits.

And they did **not** have a boy. They had a girl named Muna, about the same age as Sameer. He often saw her playing in her yard, or helping her mother. But she never even looked his way.

As the weather cooled, the green olives started to ripen. Some fell to the ground, and as usual, Sameer gathered them in a basket.

One morning he noticed Muna standing at the wall, watching him. At last she spoke.

"Those are our olives, you know. Ours!"

Sameer faced her. "They're on our land," he said.

"But the tree is on **our** land," said Muna. "It has belonged to my family for a hundred years."

Yes, that was true. The old tree stood firmly on Muna's side of the wall. Over the years, however, some of its branches had twisted and bent until they stretched far across the wall. They dropped the best olives in Lebanon on Sameer's side.

"Listen," said Sameer. "All the time you people were away, we took care of this tree. We have a right to the olives."

"But now we're back," said Muna, "and **we'll** take care of it. **We'll** have the olives."

Sameer scowled at Muna. Then he leaned over the wall, dumped his basket of olives into her yard, and walked away.

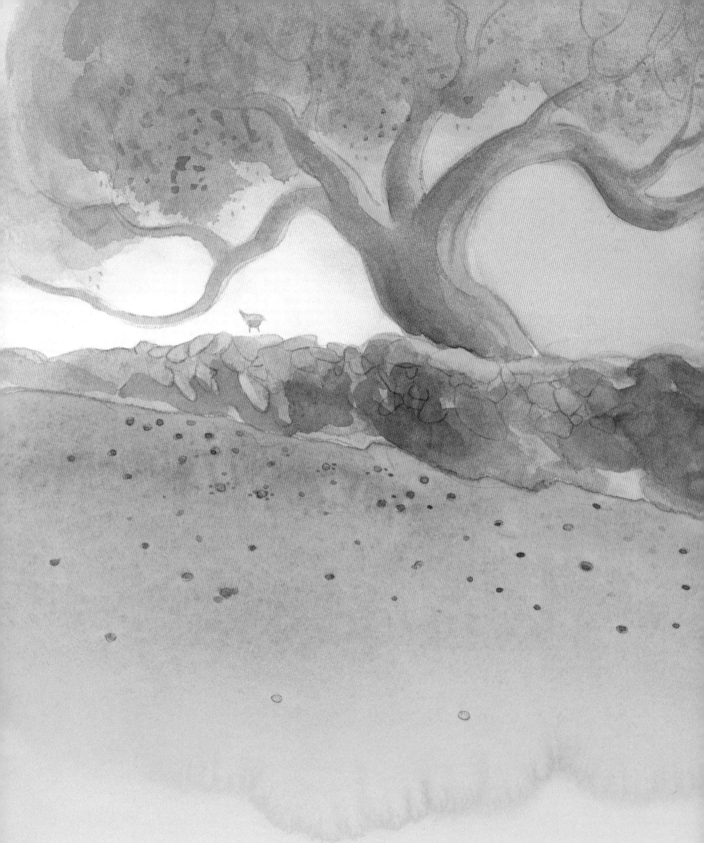

After that, the olives went on dropping in Sameer's yard . . .

but nobody ever gathered them.

One night a fierce autumn storm rolled over the mountains, with blazing lightning and booms of thunder.

One terrible bolt seemed to shake the whole world. At daybreak Sameer rushed outside to see what had happened.

The olive tree was gone. Nothing was left but a shattered stump. Pieces of pale wood lay scattered all over the two yards. Even the stone wall was broken.

Sameer and his family stood on their side,
and Muna and her family stood on theirs.
No one spoke as they gazed at the remains
of the tree.

After a while, the
grownups drifted sadly
back into their houses.

Sameer's eyes were stinging. How he would miss that tree!

Then he noticed Muna still standing in her yard. Slowly she came over to the broken stump of the tree. Sameer started to leave—but as she began to speak, he paused.

"They always told me about this tree," Muna said quietly. "It seemed to me like our home, which we nearly lost. And now it's gone."

Sameer wanted to tell her, *Your family didn't have to go away. You could have stayed here, and we would have been friends—and have shared the olives.*

But it would do no good to say that now. Instead, Sameer looked around at the scraps of wood, strewn all over the yards of both families. They would have a big job, he thought, cleaning up all that wood.

Again he started toward his house. But once more he paused and looked back. Muna was still there. And that made Sameer think of one last thing he could do for his old friend the olive tree.

"Well," he said to Muna, "at least you'll have plenty of firewood this winter."

Sameer picked up a couple of the large chunks lying in his yard, stepped over the broken wall, and laid them next to Muna's house. Back and forth he went, carrying the wood to Muna's yard. Then, turning, he stopped short in surprise.

Muna had gone over to Sameer's yard. There, she too was picking up pieces of wood—and she was piling them by his house.

So the two kept working, each in the other's yard. Without words, they cleared up the olive wood, each stacking it neatly against the other's house.

As Sameer worked, another idea came to him. Maybe they could plant a new olive tree by the wall . . . a tree that both families could share?

Finally Sameer went home. And there, on a chair by the door, was a pile of perfect olives, carefully saved from among the withering leaves.